OLIVIA™
the Princess

adapted by Natalie Shaw
based on the screenplay written by Kent Redeker
illustrated by Shane L. Johnson

Simon Spotlight
New York   London   Toronto   Sydney

Based on the TV series *OLIVIA*™ as seen on Nickelodeon™

SIMON SPOTLIGHT
An imprint of Simon & Schuster Children's Publishing Division
1230 Avenue of the Americas, New York, New York 10020
Copyright © 2011 Silver Lining Productions Limited (a Chorion company).
All rights reserved. OLIVIA™ and © 2011 Ian Falconer. All rights reserved.
All rights reserved, including the right of reproduction in whole or in part in any form.
SIMON SPOTLIGHT and colophon are registered trademarks of Simon & Schuster, Inc.
For information about special discounts for bulk purchases, please contact
Simon & Schuster Special Sales at 1-866-506-1949 or business@simonandschuster.com.
Manufactured in the United States of America 0711 LAK
First Edition 1 2 3 4 5 6 7 8 9 10
ISBN 978-1-4424-3033-4

Olivia, Francine, and Daisy were playing princess when Mom rushed in with exciting news. The royal family of Poshtonia was coming to town to visit their vacation castle, and everyone was invited to greet them at the airport!

"A real king and queen?" asked Olivia.

"And a real princess, Princess Stephanie," added Mom.

The next day everyone cheered as the royal airplane rolled to a stop, but Olivia was pushed to the back of the crowd and couldn't see. In a flash the princess climbed into the royal carriage behind the king and queen, and it sped away. "The princess was so beautiful!" said Francine. "Did you see that dress?"
"I saw her back, I think," said Olivia.

On the way home, Dad and Mom tried to cheer Olivia up.

"Well, do you know what's even better than princesses?" Dad asked.

"Cherry chocolate chunk ice cream!" Olivia said.

"That's just what I was thinking," said Dad.

They drove to the ice-cream parlor. Just as they were about to go inside they heard someone ask for help. It was the king of Poshtonia!

"It seems our carriage has broken a wheel, but none of us knows how to fix it," said the king.

"Well, Mr. King, sir, I think I can help," Dad said. He turned to Mom and the queen. "This could take a while. Maybe *your highnesses* would like to take everyone inside for some ice cream?"

"Did someone say ice cream?" said a voice coming from the carriage. Olivia gasped. It was Princess Stephanie! As they headed inside, Olivia and the princess stared at each other.

"You look just like me!" they both said.

The princess had freckles and Olivia's ears were bigger, but other than that they could have been twins!

As soon as they ordered their ice cream, Olivia asked Princess Stephanie what it was like to be a real princess. "What do you do first in the morning?" she asked. "Ride a pony or have tea?"

The princess was about to answer when she spilled a tiny drop of ice cream onto her royal dress.

"My dress!" she said. "A princess must never have a messy dress."

"I'll help you clean up," said Olivia.

"I bet you get to wear pretty dresses like this to fancy balls," said Olivia. "I've never even been to a ball!"

"Well, you get to go to school and play with other children," replied Princess Stephanie. "I wish I could do that, even for a day."

Then Olivia had an idea. "We look so much alike. We should switch places for the day!" she suggested.

The princess was thinking the same thing! They quickly changed into each other's clothes and agreed to have their parents bring them back to the ice-cream parlor the following night, so they could switch back again.

When it was time for everyone to go home, the king thanked Olivia's dad for helping him fix the carriage wheel.

"Getting my hands dirty was most thrilling!" said the king.

"It's been a pleasure, your majesty!" said Olivia's dad as he bowed.

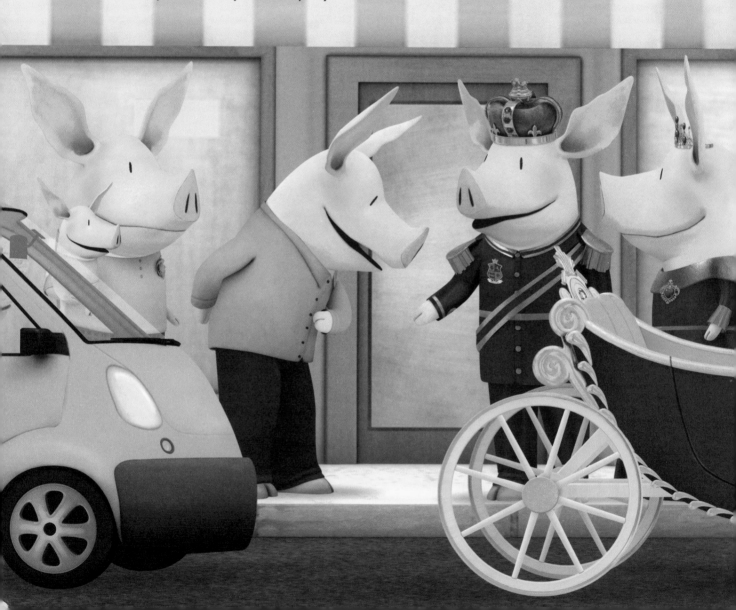

"See you later, *Olivia*!" Olivia said as she climbed into the royal carriage, dressed in Princess Stephanie's purple gown.

"Ta-ta, *Princess Stephanie*," said Princess Stephanie as she climbed into Olivia's family's car, dressed in Olivia's red clothes.

They were on their way! Olivia went to the castle to spend a day as a princess, and Princess Stephanie went to Olivia's house to spend a day as a regular girl.

When they arrived at the castle, Olivia was in awe. There were turrets and towers and even a drawbridge!

She rode Duchess the pony across the royal lawn, slid down the royal banister, and had a royal tea party.

She even had her own butler!

"I wonder if Princess Stephanie is having as much fun being me, as I am being her?" Olivia thought.

Back at Olivia's house, Princess Stephanie played fetch with Perry and banged on the drums.

"Look at me. I'm getting dirty and making noise!" she said. "How marvelous!"

When Olivia's family sat down for dinner, Princess Stephanie asked if they would be having pheasant on a silver platter. Mom laughed and set down a paper plate with a sandwich on it.

"A sandwich! On a paper plate!" said Princess Stephanie, with a big smile. "How delightful!"

After a long day it was time for Olivia and Princess Stephanie to go to bed. They both missed their real parents very much, but they knew that they would be back home soon.

At the castle the next morning, the queen announced that they had to return home to Poshtonia sooner than planned.

"But we have to go to the ice-cream parlor tonight after dinner!" said Olivia. If they couldn't go to the ice-cream parlor as planned, Olivia needed to find a way to get Princess Stephanie back to castle so they could switch places again.

"Let's have a going-away party before we leave!" she said. "We could invite that nice girl from the ice-cream parlor, and my—I mean—*her* whole class, too!" The queen agreed and sent the royal butler to deliver invitations to Olivia's classmates and their families.

Before long, the guests arrived and the going-away party was in full swing. Olivia was happy to see her friends, but it wasn't very much fun because they thought she was Princess Stephanie. She was ready to be Olivia again!

When the clock struck four, the king and queen announced that it was time to go home to Poshtonia, but Olivia's family hadn't arrived yet. Olivia knew that if she didn't speak now, she'd have to go back to Poshtonia with the royal family.

"There's something I have to tell you," she said. "I'm Olivia, not Princess Stephanie! We switched places. Look, I have bigger ears and no freckles and I'm wearing red-and-white stockings."

The queen let out a gasp. "Princess! You're not wearing purple!" she said.
"This jest has gone on long enough. We have to get on our plane. Now, pledge
to me that you'll behave like a proper princess," said the king.
That reminded Olivia of the Princess Pledge that she had made up.
"That's it! The Princess Pledge!" she said to Francine and Daisy.
"There's no such thing as a princess pledge," said the queen.

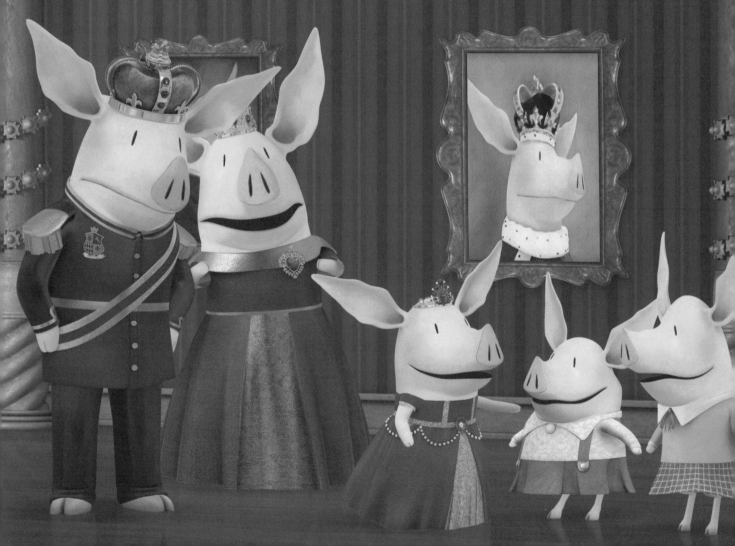

"Maybe not in Poshtonia," Olivia said. "But there is one here in Maywood!"
Olivia began to say the Princess Pledge, and Francine and Daisy joined in. "A princess promises to be pretty, peppy, smell nice, sparkle a lot, sing happy songs very loudly, and never, ever be mean."
When they finished the pledge, Francine smiled and gave Olivia a big hug.
"Olivia! It really *is* you!" she said. "But if you are the real Olivia, where is the real Princess Stephanie?"

It turned out that Olivia's family's car had a flat tire, which is why they didn't make it to the party. The king leaned out of the carriage and asked Dad if he could use some help. As soon as the carriage stopped, Olivia and Princess Stephanie ran into their mothers' arms.

"Mom," said Olivia. "I missed you!"

"Mumsy," said Princess Stephanie, running to the queen. "I missed you ever so much!"

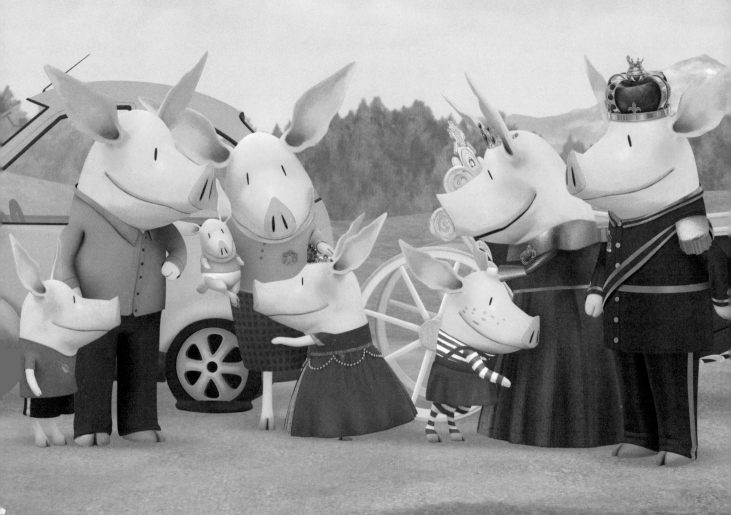

Olivia's mom was confused. Then the queen explained that the girls had switched places for a day, and it all made sense. Before long, it was time for Olivia and Princess Stephanie to say good-bye.

"I had so much fun being you," Princess Stephanie said to Olivia.

"And it was *really* fun pretending to be you," said Olivia. "Let's be friends forever!"

That night at bedtime, the real Princess Stephanie told the queen about her amazing day.

"I played with the dog, and I ate a sandwich on a paper plate. . . . ," she said.

At Olivia's house, the real Olivia told her mom all about her time at the castle.

"I rode a pony and had a tea party and even wore purple pajamas!" she said.

Their moms gave them a kiss and tucked them in tight, happy to have their daughters at home.

"It's good to be home," Olivia and Princess Stephanie said.

"Good night, my little princess," their moms said. "Sweet dreams!"

And *both* little princesses fell fast asleep.